A Really Popular Girl

A Really Popular Girl

Kathryn Ewing

AN
APPLE
PAPERBACK

SCHOLASTIC INC.
New York Toronto London Auckland Sydney

0-590-43202-8

12 11 10 9 8 7 6 5 4 3 2 1   9/8 0 1 2 3 4/9

Printed in the U.S.A.   28

To all Sheldons everywhere
with love

1

Everyone was laughing at her.

Even as Marcy woke up and found herself safe in her new bed in her new room in the new house on Dell Lane, the jeering laughter stayed in her ears. She must have done something awful to make these kids whom she didn't know and had never seen before in her life laugh at her that way. She squeezed her eyes shut tight and tried to get back into the dream to find out what she had done. But now she was wide awake.

It was too late to go back to sleep anyway. A bright September sun was shining through her window, heralding her first day in the fifth grade of the John Wellington Elementary School. From down in the kitchen she could hear her mother singing as she fixed breakfast. From the master bedroom came her stepfather's cheery whistle.

And why shouldn't they whistle and sing? Her mother and Mr. Compton, her stepfather, didn't have to get on a strange bus with a lot of people they didn't know, and get driven to a strange school where they would be held captive for six hours before being brought home again. Why shouldn't they be happy?

The mocking laughter surged back through her, making her blood run cold, because she remembered her dream now. Not the whole dream, but parts of it. She had gotten on the school bus and somebody had stuck out a foot and tripped her — some boy, some older kid, and everybody had laughed. When she got up, he held out his foot and tripped her again.

But that wasn't the worst part. The worst part was when she dreamed she was all alone walking down this empty hall in her new school. The bell had rung, and the doors to all the classrooms were closed. Through the window panels on the doors she could see kids sitting at their desks and she could hear the teachers' voices, but she didn't know which room she was supposed to be in. She kept walking and walking, and the hall kept getting longer and longer. There were no more classrooms or kids or teachers. She heard footsteps behind her, so she started to walk more quickly. The footsteps quickened, too, and she started to run so fast she couldn't catch her breath. That was when she had woken up, heart pounding.

Now there was a tap at her door. "Rise and shine, Marcy," Mr. Compton called out. "Rise and shine."

Her step always said "Rise and shine." He also always said "incidentally": "Incidentally, it's beginning to rain." "Incidentally, I need some shaving cream." "Incidentally, I'll be late getting home for dinner tonight." Things like that.

After her mother got married to Mr. Compton last June and they moved away from Glenview and into this new house in Linden Acres, her mother began saying "incidentally," too.

Marcy had even begun saying it herself. "Incidentally," she announced, when she got dressed and went downstairs to the kitchen, "incidentally, I feel like I'm going to throw up in school."

"Nonsense, Marcia!" Mr. Compton cried. "You're going to be fine. Just fine."

She knew Mr. Compton meant well, but she was grateful when her mother said, "Marcy, I want you to sit right down and slowly chew up little bites of bread and wash them down with sips of water. That's a trick I've learned. When I feel sick, it always makes me feel better."

Marcy began chewing small bits of bread and washing them down with water. After all, her mother should know what she was talking about. Her mother felt sick lots of times these days, because she was pregnant and was going to have a baby.

Marcy soon felt full with all that bread and water sloshing around in her stomach. But the trick must have worked because she didn't feel sick anymore. Still, she really wished she didn't have to go to school, and after Mr. Compton left for work she said as much.

"Marcy, you know all children have to go to school," her mother replied.

"I mean today," Marcy said. She certainly knew children had to go to school. "I wish I could wait till tomorrow."

"And have all this to do over again?" her mother exclaimed softly. "Why, anticipation is the hardest part. Once you step on that school bus and are on your way, the worst will be over."

Marcy remembered her dream — the boy tripping her on the school bus; the long, empty hall. "The worst won't be over!" she declared hotly. "The worst will just be starting! All those new kids . . . ! New teachers . . . ! I won't know where to go, what to do!"

Mrs. Compton continued to stack breakfast dishes in the dishwasher, not even bothering to look around at her daughter; in Marcy's view this was all her fault. If her mother hadn't married Mr. Compton they would still be living in Glenview, just the two of them, and Marcy would still be going to good old Kingswood Elementary.

"Someone will help you, Marcy," her mother said.

"Who?" Marcy asked miserably.

"Lots of people." Mrs. Compton glanced up at the kitchen clock. "It's getting late. You'd better be on your way."

As soon as her mother said this, it felt as if streaks of lightning were shooting through Marcy. She thought maybe she was even dreaming again. But she wasn't. Her mother was looking at her with that worried little frown she always got when Marcy was sick or when something was really wrong.

"Suppose I walk you down to the corner and wait for the bus with you," she said, adding quickly, "just for today, I mean."

"Mom, no!" Marcy wailed. She couldn't imagine anything worse than having all those kids on the school bus see that her mother had to wait with her.

5

Mrs. Compton sighed. "Well, *what* then?"

Was her mother weakening? Marcy's heart gave a leap. Tomorrow was a whole twenty-four hours away. Maybe by tomorrow she'd feel different. Maybe she would even *want* to go to John Wellington Elementary School. "*Please*, Mom . . . ?" she begged.

For a moment hope spun in the air. Then her mother said, "What will you tell your dad when he calls tonight? If you don't go, I mean."

Suddenly Marcy knew she would have to go.

Her father lived with his wife, Ginny, out in San Francisco. Tonight he would be calling clear across the country just to ask Marcy how she had made out in her new school. How could she tell him she hadn't had the guts to go?

She rose from the table and slung the strap of her handbag over her shoulder. "I'd better get a move on," she said, "or I'll miss the bus."

2

The letter that had come from the John Wellington Elementary School stated that students living on Dell Lane would be picked up by the school bus on the northeast corner of Crescent Drive and Dell Lane at approximately 8:10 A.M. These students were assigned to the Blue bus. Enclosed with the letter was the blue card which Marcy now carried in her hand.

As she approached the corner of Crescent Drive and Dell Lane, she saw another kid holding a blue card. This kid, a boy, stood beside a senior citizen lady who wore a pants suit and was smoking a cigarette.

"Hi," the senior citizen said. "I'm Mrs. Weissman, and this is my grandson, Sheldon Weissman-Cobb. Sheldon has come to live with me. This is his first day at the John Wellington Elementary School. I see you're on the Blue bus, too. What's your name?"

"Marcy Benson," Marcy replied.

"And where do you live, Marcy?"

"At 15 Dell Lane."

"Sheldon lives right there," Mrs. Weissman said, turning and pointing to the house behind her. "He doesn't know anybody around here, yet."

"Neither do I," Marcy said.

"Don't tell me you're new here, too!" the woman exclaimed. "What grade are you in?"

When Marcy told her the fifth grade, she turned to her grandson. "Well, there," she said happily. "There you are, Sheldon. Both in the same grade, how about that?" She turned back to Marcy. "Sheldon is a little nervous starting off this morning. He's afraid he might get sick."

Marcy looked at Sheldon more closely. He looked sick. His face was really white. She wished she could tell him about little sips of water and little bites of bread, but it was too late for that. The school bus, with a big square of blue cardboard fixed to a corner of the windshield, had turned into Dell Lane.

"He'll be fine," Marcy said, sounding for all the world like her stepfather. "Just fine."

"Oh, thank you," Mrs. Weissman sighed, as though Marcy had done her a big favor. "Thank you. And will you," she said, "keep an eye on him for me?"

Marcy was really surprised, being asked to keep an eye on a kid her own age. But Sheldon looked as though he needed an eye kept on him. He was shorter than she was but stocky and his dark eyes and black curly hair made his face look really pale.

"Sure," she said, as lights started flashing and the school bus drew up to the curb.

The funny thing was, the moment Marcy started thinking about Sheldon being nervous, she no longer felt nervous herself.

"Here, Sheldon, sit here," she said, slipping into the first empty seats they came to.

The bus was almost full, and noisy. Sheldon sat down beside her. Couldn't he speak? So far, he hadn't said a single word. "Anticipation is the hardest part," Marcy told him, remembering how her mother had tried to reassure her.

"*Anticipation!*" said Sheldon. "That's a big word."

Marcy looked at him. He had this little smile on his face. Was he making fun of her? She jerked her head away.

"Anticipation: a-n-t-i-c-i-p-a-t-i-o-n," Sheldon continued, spelling it out. "Right? Am I right?"

Wrong! Marcy longed to say. But she didn't, because she wasn't really sure.

This didn't stop Sheldon. "I bet you don't know, and that's why you're not saying." He spelled it out again. "A-n-t-i-c-i-p-a-t-i-o-n. Your word for today."

Marcy stared out the window. One thing was sure: Sheldon Cobb didn't need anybody to keep an eye on him. That grandmother of his had a lot to learn.

When the bus reached the school and they all piled out, Sheldon followed right at her heels. It made Marcy mad to have him breathing down her neck. But when she wasn't sure which way to turn, he said, "We go this way," and sure enough, he was right.

He also was right when he said, as though she couldn't read her own name, "There you are. Marcia Benson. There's your desk."

The desks in Mr. Willis's fifth grade had small, neatly lettered signs on them. Marcy was happy to see that Sheldon would be seated some distance away from her, three desks ahead and in the next aisle. She was also happy to see that a girl who had gotten on the bus at Myrtle Way was in her room. The girl looked really nice. And

Myrtle Way was just the next street over from Dell Lane. Marcy listened hard when Mr. Willis read out his list of names. The girl's name was Alison Bamforth.

When Mr. Willis read out "Sheldon Cobb," right away Sheldon's hand shot up.

"Correction," Sheldon said. "Weissman-Cobb. It's a hyphenated name."

"Excuse me, Sheldon," Mr. Willis said, and made a mark on his list. "Sheldon Weissman-hyphenated-Cobb."

Marcy thought Mr. Willis spoke a lot more politely than Sheldon Weissman-hyphenated-Cobb.

After Mr. Willis got finished with his list of names, he told them about the rules: Only one person talks at a time; raise your hand if you have something to say; get a pass to go through the halls during classes.

Hurry up, Mr. Willis, hurry up! Marcy silently begged. If only she hadn't taken all those little sips of water!

As soon as Mr. Willis stopped talking, Marcy hurried to the front of the room and asked for a pass to go to the girls' room. She had no problem going through the halls or finding her way back to her classroom. It seemed foolish now to have dreamed otherwise.

When she came back, she made herself walk past Alison Bamforth's desk.

"Hi," she said, giving Alison a small smile.

Marcy felt she couldn't have lived with herself if she hadn't had the courage to do that.

3

Lunch was in the cafeteria from 12:15 to 12:45 P.M. You could bring your lunch or buy it. Marcy didn't know which she wanted to do yet, so her mother had given her money to buy lunch the first day.

When it got close to lunchtime she started worrying about who she could eat with. But when the bell rang, there was Alison Bamforth standing at her desk.

"Hi," Alison said. "You're new here, aren't you? Would you like to eat with us?"

Marcy was so relieved and happy she had to blink to keep tears from coming to her eyes. "Yes," she said.

She walked through the crowded hall beside Alison without knowing where she was going or what she was saying. She was trying so hard to act just right that she was giving herself a pain in the head. Or maybe this was caused by the noise in the cafeteria, which was enough to give anybody a pain in the head.

"Wellington has a telephone service called Tip Line," Alison explained. "We take turns phoning into it each night to find out what the cafeteria will be serving the next day. If we don't like it, then we bring our lunch. But today is spaghetti, so we're all having that."

Following Alison, Marcy picked up a tray and got into the cafeteria line.

Kids kept calling out to Alison all the time, saying hi. Marcy could see Alison was not only pretty and nice. She was a really popular girl.

When they got their spaghetti and cartons of milk, Alison led the way to a table. Three girls were already seated there, two of them from Mr. Willis's homeroom.

"This is Marcia Benson," Alison said. "She used to live in Glenview."

Alison introduced the girls: Tish Chandlor, Nina Hernandez, Diana Flynn.

"Glenview!" Tish Chandlor exclaimed. "Do you know Wendy Howard? She lives in Glenview. She's my cousin."

"Wendy Howard was my best Glenview friend," Marcy cried.

Having Wendy for a friend really seemed to help break the ice. Marcy began to breathe easier, and the pain left her head.

In the schoolyard after lunch, kids were talking in groups and playing games and having fun. But Marcy noticed that Sheldon wasn't doing anything. He was just standing off by himself, looking around.

If anybody had told Marcy when she woke up that morning that by the time the school bus dropped her off that afternoon she would have made four friends at the John Wellington Elementary School, she wouldn't have believed them.

"How was it?" her mother asked as soon as she came in the back door.

"Mom, it was great!" she said. "It's a really nice school, and Mr. Willis is a neat teacher. But the best part is, there are these four girls that are my friends."

"Four friends already, Marcy!" her mother exclaimed.

It interested Marcy to see that when her mother was happy she had to blink back tears, too.

*   *   *

Over the telephone that night, her father said, "I knew you'd do it, Marcy! I knew you'd come through!"

When he said this, Marcy could picture in her mind just how he looked. He would be standing at the telephone in the kitchen way out in California, one leather boot hitched up on a chair, his blue eyes smiling and glittery. Thinking of him real clear that way made her miss him so much she couldn't speak.

"Marcy?" he said. "Marcy? Are you still there?"

"Sure," she managed.

"Well, so tell me about your teacher. Tell me about your subjects. What are you taking? English? Social Studies? Math?"

After Marcy got through telling him all about school, even about the spaghetti she had had for lunch, her father's voice kind of changed and he said, "I've got some news, too."

"What?" Marcy asked.

"Well," her father said, "Ginny is going to have a baby."

Marcy was surprised. "Ginny is going to have a baby?"

"Sometime in March."

"March! That's when Mom is having her baby!"

It was really something. Come March, she

16

would have not one but two new relations. "Do you want a girl or a boy?" she asked.

"Ginny and I don't much care which it is."

Marcy nodded. "As long as it's healthy. That's what Mom and Step keep saying. But I hope one of you has a boy, and one a girl. That way, I'll have one half brother, and one half sister." She wondered if one of them might turn out to look like her — on the skinny side with straight brown hair and kind of light brown eyes.

It was really interesting the way her family was adding up. Last year there had been just her mother and herself living at 9 Morris Avenue in Glenview, and her father living out in San Francisco.

Now there was her father's new wife, Ginny, who was her stepmother; Ginny's little kid, Joey, who was her stepbrother; her mother's new husband, Mr. Compton, who was her stepfather; Mr. Compton's son, Roger, out in Denver, Colorado, who was her Compton stepbrother; Roger's sister, Carole Anne, who was her Compton stepsister — and that was not counting the two brandnew relatives who would be arriving in March.

"By March," she told her father, "I'm going to be related to nine people."

"That's a bunch," said her father.

17

"It sure is." A thought struck her. "What do you figure on naming yours?"

"We haven't decided yet."

"I'm thinking up some names for Mom and Step. I'll start thinking up some for you and Ginny, if you want me to."

"That'll be fine."

"How about Benjamin, if it's a boy? After Benjamin Franklin."

"Benjamin Benson?"

She could tell he didn't like it. "I'll work on it."

"Do that," he said, and then, "Well, Marcy. . . ."

When he said it like that, it meant he was getting ready to hang up, and right away Marcy felt her throat tighten. She tried to think of things to say to keep talking longer. "Tell Ginny I'm glad about the baby."

"I will," he promised.

"And tell Joey I said hello."

"I will."

"What's he doing now?"

"Who? Joey?"

"Yes."

Her father gave a laugh so warm and deep and like himself that tears started to fill her eyes. "Marcy, you know there's a time difference out here. It's still afternoon. Joey's at home, and I'm at the store."

18

"At the store? So how's business?" she persisted. "Sell any good stamps lately?"

"Not lately."

Her father was the owner and operator of Benson's, Inc., specializing in rare stamps and coins. When she went out to visit him, he let her go to work with him sometimes.

"How are Miss Sullivan and Mr. Cotter?"

Miss Sullivan and Mr. Cotter worked in the store.

"They're both fine, Marcy. I'll tell them you said hello. Now I'd better get back to work. And I guess you've got homework to do."

Marcy could tell he was getting impatient, wanting to hang up. This made her so mad she didn't feel like talking to him at all. If he was going to act like he was in such a hurry, why didn't he just say good-bye? She clamped her lips shut tight and let the silence go buzzing out across the entire country, across the whole U.S. of A.

"Marcy . . . ?" he said. "I'll call you again next week, okay?"

Still she let the silence buzz.

"Okay?"

"Okay," she said at last, because she knew it was his turn to start getting mad.

"Next week, then," he said. "And Marcy," he

added, "going into a new school isn't easy. I'm proud of you."

Suddenly, the missing him was too much. Tears started rolling down her cheeks and getting into her mouth. She could taste salt on her tongue. "Dad," she said, "I love you."

4

As soon as Marcy hung up from talking to her father, the telephone rang right away. It was for her again. This time it was Alison Bamforth.

"Hot dogs and sauerkraut tomorrow," Alison said. "So bring your lunch."

Marcy happened to like hot dogs and sauerkraut, but she dried her eyes on her shirt and said "sure" real fast.

"And," Alison added, "we're starting up the *Linden Acres Express* again. Everybody wants you to be on it. If you want to be, that is."

"Sure!" Marcy said, even though she didn't know what the *Linden Acres Express* was all about, or who "everybody" was.

"Good," Alison said. "We're having a meeting at my house tomorrow after school. By the way, everybody likes you a lot."

The next morning, Marcy found Sheldon Weissman-hyphenated-Cobb already standing on the corner waiting for the school bus.

"How come you're bringing your lunch?" he asked, eyeing her brown paper lunch bag.

"Because they're having sauerkraut and hot dogs today," she told him.

"What's wrong with sauerkraut and hot dogs?"

"We don't like them."

He got this little smile on his face. "Who's we? All your new friends?"

Marcy decided to ignore him, but this was difficult because he went right on talking.

"Did you do that footprint thing?" he asked. "That thing Wee Willis Winkie told us to write?"

Calling Mr. Willis "Wee Willis Winkie" was pretty funny, even if it wasn't very polite. Marcy had to suck in her cheeks real hard to keep from giving Sheldon the satisfaction of seeing that he could make her laugh. "Yes," she said.

"How many pages did you write?"

Mr. Willis had asked the class to write a story about where footprints might be going to or coming from. Marcy had imagined her own footprints leaving Kingswood Elementary School in Glenview and arriving at the John Wellington Elementary School in Linden Acres. She had been pleased with the idea and had taken great pains with it. "I wrote two whole pages."

"Two!" Sheldon cried. "I wrote six! Want to know what mine is about?"

"No," Marcy told him.

"It's really good."

"I bet."

"No kidding. My mom's a writer. She lives in New York City. I take after her. Mine is called 'The Invisible Footprint.' "

"How can it be a footprint if it's invisible?"

"See?" Sheldon exclaimed in triumph. "Right away, I've got you wondering. Right away, there's interest."

"There is not," said Marcy. "And here comes the bus."

Marcy sought out the same seat she had taken yesterday, and Sheldon plopped down beside her.

"I'll tell you about my story," he said. "There's this big green animal roaming all around the neighborhood, see."

"Green?" Marcy said absently. She was keeping a sharp eye out, watching for Alison to get on at Myrtle Way so she could be sure to wave to her.

"Ah, yes," said Sheldon, observing the two girls' little exchange of greeting. "The ritual morning salutation. That's *s-a-l-u-t-a-t-i-o-n*. Your new word for the day."

Marcy glared at him. "Do you always talk like that?"

"Only to those I consider intelligent. Like you, Marcy." He smiled. "Now to get back to my story. There is this great big animal roaming around the neighborhood, a killer animal that eats dogs, cats — everything. At night people hear cats screeching, dogs yelping in pain. In the morning they find blood and mangled pieces of flesh and fur on their patios, and in the streets. And the police are all looking for this killer. But he can't be found. You know why?"

"Because," Marcy answered patiently, "of his invisible footprint."

"Aha! But *why* is his footprint invisible? Can you tell me that?"

"Sheldon, I don't happen to care why."

"Lack of curiosity is a sign of stupidity, Marcia. Maybe you're not as intelligent as I thought. Anyway, the reason nobody can find him is because he's a new phenomenon. He wasn't born. He grew, like a vegetable, or a plant. And instead of animal fur, he's got this great, thick, green pelt of grass on him, a coat of green grass that lets him sink right down into somebody's nice green lawn and be invisible every time he sees the police

24

coming around. How do you like that? An animal the size of a big dog, like a Saint Bernard or something, with this thick coat of green grass rippling across his back. . . ."

It *was* a good story. Even though Sheldon was such a show-off, Marcy had to admit that much. "So then what happens?" she asked.

"AstroTurf," said Sheldon.

"AstroTurf?"

"The police are after him, see? And he runs past this football stadium and spies the green AstroTurf. He thinks it's nice green grass and he runs in and tries to sink down and hide in it, but he can't. The police have him cornered and blast him." He shook his head. "AstroTurf . . . What a thought! What a thought!"

They had arrived at the school. The bus stopped and kids were getting off, but Sheldon didn't budge.

Marcy poked him. "Sheldon," she whispered. "Come on, Sheldon, get up. We're here."

Sheldon looked out the window in surprise. "Why, so we are," he said. "So we are."

Marcy sighed. Sheldon did need keeping an eye on. Maybe his grandmother was right.

Just before lunch Mr. Willis said, "I've looked over some of the compositions you turned in this morning. One of them captures what it's like to have to leave your old school and go to a new school, and I'd like to read it to you."

Mr. Willis smiled at Marcy, and Marcy felt her heart start to pound.

"This composition is entitled 'Changes,' " he continued. "It's by Marcy Benson.

" 'When I think about footsteps leaving a place or coming to a place, I think of leaving Kingswood Elementary School in Glenview, and coming to the John Wellington Elementary School in Linden Acres.

" 'At first, my footsteps were sad because of all the friends that I wouldn't see anymore, and because of all the teachers I liked, and things like that. I thought I would just hate my new school, and all the kids and teachers and everything. Or maybe not hate, but just not like it very well.

" 'But my footsteps carried me through the door of the John Wellington Elementary School, and I already like it a whole lot. It is a wonderful school with nice teachers and kids who are really friendly.

" 'So if you ever find out that you have to leave your old school and go to a new one, just remember this story and you will know that anticipation may be the worst part. The End.' "

Mr. Willis looked up. "I'm sure we all have a good idea now of how it feels to have to leave one school and go to another. I would just like to add that Marcia's paper is very neatly written, and the spelling is perfect, including the word *anticipation*." He looked around the room. "Is there anyone else here, I wonder, who can spell that word?"

Right away, Sheldon's hand shot up. Marcy wasn't surprised.

5

There were two types of houses in Linden Acres: colonial and ranch.

Tish Chandlor, Nina Hernandez, and Alison Bamforth lived in ranch houses; and Diana Flynn lived in a colonial like Marcy's.

Diana had two older brothers. Nina had two younger sisters. Tish Chandlor was an only child, Alison had a brother on each side of her; she called them "The Bookends."

The girls, all five of them, sat on the floor around the big coffee table in the Bamforths' family room. It was the meeting of the *Linden Acres Express* that Alison had invited Marcy to attend. On the table were several copies of past editions of the newspaper. The girls had written it out with felt-tip pens on lined notebook paper, duplicated the pages on a copy machine, and stapled them together.

Alison had said they should all get to know one another before they got down to business, which was how Marcy found out about everybody's brothers and sisters. Now Alison was smiling and saying, "Marcy, what about you?"

It seemed to Marcy that everyone already knew all about everyone else, except, of course, for her. "I have a little stepbrother out in San Francisco," she explained. "He lives with his mom and my dad. And I have a stepbrother and a stepsister my age, who live with their mom in Denver, Colorado."

She decided not to mention the expected arrival of the two new half relatives in March. Her family seemed complicated enough.

"I live with my mom and my stepfather mostly," she finished. "But in the summer, I visit with my dad."

"Ooooh! You poor thing!" Nina Hernandez wailed. "Oooh, I feel so sorry for you! Every time my parents have a fight, I think they're going to get a divorce and I cry my eyes out."

Marcy could see Nina was really upset. "It's not so bad," she said, trying to be cheerful. Who knew? Maybe one day Nina would find herself in the same boat Marcy was in now.

"How do you like them?" Nina pressed. "Your steps, I mean."

"They're okay."

"Okay good, or okay bad?"

Marcy thought of Ginny out in San Francisco, getting ready to have her new baby. She thought of Mr. Compton whistling as he shaved in the morning. "Okay good, I guess."

"Ooooh, I never would!" cried Nina. "I'd hate having steps. It would be the worst thing in the world."

"Nina, there are lots of worse things than that," declared Tish Chandlor. "How about if your parents got some disease?"

"How about if they burned to death in an airplane crash?" demanded Diana. "How about nuclear war?"

Everybody began talking all at once, shouting about the worst things that could happen, until Alison picked up her father's hammer, which she used to call the meetings to order, and pounded it on a block of wood. "I make a motion we stop making Marcia feel bad just because her parents are divorced," she said. "All in favor say aye."

Everybody said "aye," and looked contritely at Marcy, who did her best to look forgiving and brave.

"Now let's get to work," Alison said. "What shall we use for my 'Dear Alison' column this month?"

Diana began to giggle. " 'Dear Alison,' " she said, " 'I'm always losing my false teeth. What should I do?' Signed, 'Forgetful.' "

" 'Dear Forgetful,' " Tish cried out. " 'Try putting them in with glue.' "

"No, no, I've got a better one!" exclaimed Nina. "How about, 'Dear Alison, The girl behind me is always talking in school. What should I do?' Signed, 'Wants Quiet.' And the answer is, 'Dear Wants Quiet, Try teaching her sign language.' "

"Wait a minute, wait a minute!" Diana cried out. "I've got the best one!" She pressed her lips together to try to keep from laughing. "How about, 'Dear Alison, People don't hyphenate my name. What should I do?' Signed, 'Big Deal.' And the answer is, 'Dear Big Deal, Pass out pencils.' "

"No, no!" countered Tish. "How about just 'Pass out'?"

"How about 'Pass out cold and don't get up again'?" Nina yelled.

They all knew who "Big Deal" was, of course, and by this time everyone was shouting and giggling, even Alison. Marcy felt guilty, laughing along with the others, even though in a way Sheldon probably deserved it.

After Alison called the meeting to order again, they started to figure out the features.

"Sports!" Diana cried. "I want to do sports. My brothers can help me."

"Not boys' sports," objected Tish Chandlor. "Girls' sports."

"Soccer, then," Diana amended.

"Not many girls play soccer." It was Tish again.

"Soccer fans!" cried Nina. "Girls can be soccer fans."

"How about, 'Soccer — Join a Team, Be a Fan,'" Alison suggested.

Marcy noticed that whenever Alison said something, people agreed with her right away.

With the sports page taken care of, they moved on to entertainment. Nina would do a TV review.

"And don't just give everything four stars all the time," Diana told her. "You're supposed to say what's wrong with shows, not just that they're good."

"That's right, Nina," Tish chimed in. "You should find some dumb shows and tell about them."

"But I don't like to watch dumb shows."

"Then you shouldn't be our TV reviewer," Diana retorted.

Marcy gulped. These girls really took the *Linden Acres Express* seriously!

Tish Chandlor would, as usual, do her comic strip, "Linden Loonies." There would also be an advertisement asking for photographs of pets, a recipe for quick spaghetti sauce, and a want ad (Paper carriers needed. Lots of fun but no pay).

"Now, Marcy," Alison said, turning to her, "what would you like to do?"

"I know!" Tish exclaimed. "She can do interviews. Marcia, who could you interview?"

The girls all looked at her. Marcy racked her brain. She had just moved to Linden Acres. She didn't know anyone. Then she heard herself say, "Sheldon Weissman-Cobb."

"Sheldon Weissman-Cobb!" Diana cried. "Why in the world would you want to interview him?"

"Well — he's new," Marcy began; adding more firmly, "and his mother is a writer. She lives in New York."

Nina perked up. "He lives here, and his mother lives in New York? How come?"

"That," Marcy said, "is what I intend to find out."

6

The next morning waiting for the school bus Marcy made an appointment to interview Sheldon for the *Linden Acres Express*. It was Sheldon who called it an "appointment."

"Sheldon is expecting you," Mrs. Weissman said, opening the front door to Marcy that afternoon. "He tells me he is to be featured in your newspaper. I'd like to order fifty copies."

Marcy's eyes widened. "Fifty copies?"

"To send to all my friends." Mrs. Weissman's hand shook as she lit a cigarette.

Marcy figured ordering so many copies made her nervous. It certainly made Marcy nervous to think her interview was going to be read by fifty of Mrs. Weissman's friends.

"Just go along down the hall, last door on your left." Mrs. Weissman said. "I have to get back to a letter I'm writing to my congressman."

Did Mrs. Weissman write to *congressmen*? Marcy was really impressed.

Going down the hall, she could see right away how Sheldon came by his interest in words. Books were everywhere — on shelves in all the rooms, on tables, on the floor, everywhere.

When she reached the last door on the left, she heard Sheldon say, "Come in, Miss Benson," and she entered what was clearly his bedroom. Sheldon sat at his desk. He motioned to a straight-backed chair pulled up beside it. "Please take a seat, Miss Benson."

Marcy sat down and opened the notebook she had brought with her. Her mother had suggested that she write down in advance the questions she wanted to ask. It was a good thing because with Sheldon acting as though she were a real reporter and he were a famous person, she could hardly keep from laughing.

"Where were you born?" she finally managed to ask.

"I was born," Sheldon replied, "in Indianapolis, Indiana, which is noted for the famous Indianapolis Speedway."

"I don't need all those extras, Sheldon."

"That's the kind of thing that lends color, Marcy. Write it down."

Marcy scribbled the words down. She would write them up her own way when she got home.

"Mother's and father's names and occupations," she said.

Sheldon frowned. "Now wait a minute, Marcy, just wait a minute. We aren't finished with residence yet. I was born in Indianapolis. Then I was taken to Cincinnati, Ohio, where my parents split up when I was five years old. I went to Providence, Rhode Island, with my mother, where I attended first and second grades. Then third grade in New Hampshire with my father, and fourth grade in New York City with my mother and her new husband." He paused, and added, "John Wellington is a new experience for me. Until I came here I went to private schools."

Marcy could scarcely believe her ears. "You've changed schools three times already?"

"She asked incredulously," Sheldon said, smiling his little smile. "Incredulously: i-n-c-r-e-d-u-l-o-u-s-l-y. Your word for the day."

Oooh! Only the fact that she wanted to be on the *Linden Acres Express* kept Marcy from leaving the Weissman residence and never coming back. "I have a word for you," she said. "Impossible."

"Spell it," Sheldon said, quick as a wink.

"I don't feel like spelling it."

"I bet you can't. I bet you don't know whether it ends in i-b-l-e or a-b-l-e."

This happened to be true, but Marcy certainly wasn't about to admit it. "One thing I do know," she declared hotly, "and that is that it's just what you are."

Sheldon gave a short laugh. "Oh, I could have told you that long ago. It's why I'm here."

Marcy didn't like to let a person as conceited as Sheldon Weissman-hyphenated-Cobb think she cared why he had come to Linden Acres. But she was curious. "What do you mean?"

"I'm here because I'm impossible. My stepfather can't stand me. He threw me out."

Who could blame him? thought Marcy. But aloud, she said, "Threw you out? Of your house?"

"Not my house, Marcia. His house. His condo, that is."

"How come?"

"He doesn't like me. But that's all right. I don't like him, either."

This interview was really getting interesting. "Why don't you like him?"

"He wants me to do everything his way."

"So what else is new?"

Grown-ups always want kids to do things their

way. Marcy thought every kid knew that. Her step had a thing about hanging your stuff in the hall closet as soon as you came in the door, and about no books or junk lying around, and about eating lots of greens.

On the other hand, her father couldn't care less about things like that. When she was living with her father out in California, she could throw her stuff around as much as she pleased. But he got really upset if she didn't at least try jellied madrilene, or didn't take advantage of new experiences like going up in a hot-air balloon even if she was scared to death.

"Why didn't you just do what your step told you to do?" she asked now.

"Why should I?"

Marcy groaned. For a smart kid, sometimes Sheldon wasn't too bright. "So you wouldn't get thrown out."

"Who cares? I wanted to get thrown out."

"I bet."

"I did! Mom and I were doing just fine till he came along."

Marcy knew what Sheldon meant. It had been like that with her and her mom. The two of them getting along fine until Mr. Compton came on the scene and whammo, everything changed.

"Maybe you just needed to get used to his ways," she offered.

"I could never get used to his ways. Never," Sheldon said.

"How come?"

"Because he's stupid, that's how come. He hasn't got a brain in his head. Do you know what he said once, Marcy? He said Bangor is the capital of the state of Maine. He also didn't know how you find the hypotenuse of a right triangle. I showed him, of course. Just as I informed him that the capital of the state of Maine is Augusta, not Bangor. But can you believe it?"

"I don't know some of those things, either," Marcy confessed, not wishing to admit her ignorance, but feeling a tug of sympathy for Sheldon's stepfather.

"But you're a child, Marcy. He's a grown-up."

"All grown-ups aren't smart, Sheldon. Everyone's different. It just depends."

"Please, Marcy, don't make excuses for him. You sound just like my mother. He doesn't need to spend all of his time exercising, lifting weights, running off to the gym. Books are available. Maps. Anyone can make an effort, anyone can be informed; anyone can get to know the capital of Maine."

"What's his name, your stepfather?"

"His name is Raymond Redfield."

"It's a nice name."

"Alliteration." Sheldon fixed her with a look. "Raymond Redfield. Nice name. A device often used in poetry."

Marcy blinked. Sometimes Sheldon seemed to be speaking a foreign language.

"My mother's poems," he said, sweeping a hand toward a collection of several slim volumes bracketed by bookends and set off by themselves on a shelf. "Those three thick books beside them are my father's philosophy studies. My father is a genius. His books have been published in four languages. He lectures all over the world."

No wonder, Marcy thought, this kid knows how to spell. With a grandmother who writes to congressmen, a mother who writes poems, and a father who is a genius, who wouldn't? "What about your dad?" she ventured. "Couldn't you go and live with him?"

"My dear Marcy," said Sheldon, "I haven't seen hide nor hair of my father since I was eight years old. Ellen Weissman is the only person who cares about me in the whole world."

"You better get her to stop smoking, then," Marcy advised.

"I know, I know!" cried Sheldon. "I worry about that all the time. Marcy, what should I do?"

Marcy gave him a look. Was he being smart again? But no, there wasn't a trace of that little smile.

7

When she got home from interviewing Sheldon, Marcy was careful to hang up her jacket in the hall closet the way Mr. Compton liked, instead of throwing it on a chair as she sometimes did.

She carried her notebook and pencil up to her bedroom and placed them neatly on her desk instead of tossing them on the kitchen counter. And at supper she ate all her salad.

But Mr. Compton didn't seem to notice. And when you came to think of it, Marcy reflected, why should he care? After all, she wasn't his kid. Why should he care whether she ate enough greens? Maybe he was tired of having her hanging around. Maybe he would even like to get rid of her, do a Raymond Redfield.

Until her interview with Sheldon, it had never occurred to Marcy that stepfathers might not be exactly overjoyed to have stepchildren living in their houses with them. But now that she thought about it, she had to ask herself what was in it for them.

"May I have some more salad, please?" she said. Marcy figured if she wanted to stay healthy she had better stop counting on Mr. Compton to check up on her, and start looking out for herself.

Her mother filled up the plate and passed it back without giving her daughter so much as a glance. Even her mother didn't seem to care whether Marcy ate enough greens. Her mother went right on talking to Mr. Compton, and it was easy to see they had only one thing on their minds — that baby her mother was going to have. Coming home from work, Mr. Compton had stopped off at a paint store and picked up a color chart. Now all they could talk about was what color they would paint the baby's room.

Finally her mother remembered that her daughter was sitting there. "What color do you think would be nice, Marcy?" she asked.

"Black," Marcy replied.

The word just popped out. She even surprised herself because all the time her mother and Mr. Compton were talking, she had been thinking of painting the baby's room a sunny yellow, and putting little decals of birds and kittens on the walls.

As soon as she said "black," her mother turned

to Mr. Compton and began talking of other things — what a warm day it had been; what would be on television that night. They didn't mention the baby's room again, and Mr. Compton put the color chart back into his pocket. Later that night, when her mother came into her room to tuck her in and kiss her good night, she sat down on the edge of the bed in the soft darkness.

"Marcy," she said, "do you really want the baby's room to be painted black?"

"No," Marcy confessed in a small voice.

"Do you have a color in mind?"

"Yellow."

"Yellow is a bright, happy color. I like that, too. Maybe we'll paint it yellow. But Marcy," her mother added, "do you have any idea why you said to paint it black?"

Marcy couldn't think of a single reason in the world why she had said a dumb thing like that. "No," she whispered.

"I think I know why," her mother said. "I think you were feeling left out, and I don't blame you. I think I'd feel left out, too, if people were making a fuss about a new baby and leaving me to feel overlooked and cast aside."

Her mother's cool hand smoothed Marcy's forehead. "I wish," she continued softly, "I could promise you'd never feel that way again. But,

Marcy, I want you always to remember that you're never left out of my heart. You have your own place there, and no one else can ever take it — not the new baby, not even Bill. You're my firstborn, and that special place belongs to you forever. Do you understand?"

"Sure," Marcy replied, because she did understand. Also, she felt like some kind of nut, saying a little baby's bedroom should be painted black. But there was something else that was bothering her. "Whose house is this?" she said.

"What's that?" her mother asked, sounding puzzled.

"Who bought this house?"

"Who bought it?"

"Yes," Marcy pressed. "Who is the owner? Does it belong to us, or to Step?"

"Why, it belongs to the three of us. It's our home because we live here."

It really got to Marcy when her mother tried to squirm out of answering a question. "You know what I mean," she said severely. "I mean, who pays the money for it?"

"Well, Bill, of course."

"Then it belongs to him, doesn't it? I mean, it doesn't belong to you."

Marcy knew she was skating on thin ice. Even in the dark she could tell her mother was frown-

45

ing. "It does belong to me, Marcy," Mrs. Compton said crisply. "The deed is in my name. My name and Bill's."

Marcy's heart took a hopeful leap. "And mine?"

"No," her mother responded more gently. "It's in my name and Bill's because we are husband and wife. We hold joint title."

Marcy didn't understand those words, but she was comforted by them. Her mother had once worked in a real estate office and therefore certainly knew what she was talking about when it came to houses. But just to be on the safe side, Marcy said, "Then if you own it, too, Step can never kick me out, right?"

"Kick you out!" her mother exclaimed. "What makes you think Bill would ever do a thing like that?"

"That's what Sheldon's step did," Marcy told her. "That's why he's living here in Linden Acres with his grandmother. Sheldon says his step can't stand him."

Her mother sat so still there in the darkness that Marcy could hear the ticking of the clock on her bureau. "I see," she said, as though at last she understood some great mystery.

"So," Marcy continued, "if Step wanted to throw me out, what would you do?"

"Marcy, that just won't happen."

Marcy sat bolt upright and caught her mother's face in both her hands. "But *if*! *If*! I said."

Gently her mother loosened Marcy's grip and held Marcy's hands in her own two firm ones. "Marcy," she said, "if such a thing were ever, ever to happen, I would leave, too. We would find someplace else to live."

Marcy was really relieved. Not that she expected anything like this to happen. The last thing Mr. Compton would want would be for her mother to leave, no matter how much her daughter threw her stuff around.

There was a tap at the door, and Mr. Compton stuck his head inside.

"What is it, Bill?" Mrs. Compton asked, sounding, Marcy thought, a bit cross at this interruption.

Mr. Compton was apologetic. "I just wanted to let you know it's time for that program we wanted to see."

"Bill, I'll be right down."

"It's starting now."

"Well, I'll be right down!"

Marcy was surprised. Her mother rarely spoke sharp and quick that way to Mr. Compton.

He pulled his head back and shut the door. Marcy's mother gave a little sigh. "I'll say good night, now," she said, leaning over and kissing

47

Marcy. Then in the doorway, she paused. "You know," she added, "when Bill looked in, here we were, all cozied up, just the two of us. I'm afraid I let him know his company wasn't wanted. I suppose there are times when he feels left out, too."

It surprised Marcy that a grown-up would feel left out. But now that she thought about it, why not?

"You better go on down, Mom," she urged.

Marcy didn't like the idea of her stepfather feeling left out. In fact, what she really liked was when her mother and Mr. Compton were both downstairs in the family room, watching television or just talking quietly together. She liked to hear their voices drifting up to her while she slipped off to sleep. Snuggling under the covers, she closed her eyes.

8

Marcy worked hard at writing up her interview with Sheldon. She checked the spelling of Indianapolis, Ohio, Rhode Island, and New Hampshire in the dictionary her father and Ginny had sent as one of their gifts to her last Christmas. But when she showed it to Sheldon a few days later at the bus stop, he took one look and frowned.

"Why isn't this typed?" he demanded.

Marcy gave kind of a squeak. "Typed?"

"Yes, Marcy. Do you suppose reporters on a big city newspaper turn in handwritten copy like this?"

"Sheldon, the *Linden Acres Express* is not a big city newspaper. Besides, none of us can type."

"You mean, not one of your friends can use a word processor? At the age of ten? Marcy, I'd be ashamed to admit that. I've been using a word processor since I was six years old."

Marcy pressed her lips together to keep from saying anything mean to someone who was able to use a word processor, but who had gotten himself kicked out of the house he lived in.

"I gather you didn't see fit to put in that background material I gave you on the Indianapolis Speedway," Sheldon continued, looking the paper over. "But at least you got in about my mother's poems and my father's books. You needn't mention my stepfather, however."

"I only said that you used to live with him in New York City."

"That was confidential, Marcy. The less said about old Reddi-Whip Redfield, the better."

"I'll erase it."

"Thank you. As for the rest, it's very nicely done." There came that smile. "I give you an A plus."

Marcy snatched the paper away from him. Who did he think he was? Mr. Willis? She looked down the street, hoping the bus would hurry up and come.

At lunch (pizza, so everyone bought), Marcy's interview got passed from hand to hand until Tish grabbed it.

" 'Sheldon Weissman-Cobb lives on Dell

Lane,' " she announced, reading aloud. " 'He has always gone to private schools until now —' "

"Big deal!" said Nina.

Diana yawned. "Who cares?"

" 'He was born,' " Tish continued, " 'in Indianapolis, Indiana, and has lived in Ohio, Rhode Island, New Hampshire, and New York. His mother has written many books of poetry. His father is a genius who has written many books. They are divorced and so he lives with his grandmother. The thing he likes best is to write stories. He says he is going to be a great and famous writer someday. It is interesting to have a boy like Sheldon living in Linden Acres.' "

"His mother writes poetry and his father writes books . . . !" Diana exclaimed.

"Are they famous?" Alison asked.

"I guess so," Marcy replied.

"Wow!" Nina breathed.

But Tish was staring at Marcy. "What got erased?"

That Tish Chandlor didn't let anything get by her.

"Just a sentence," Marcy hedged.

The girls were suddenly so quiet she could hear them breathing.

"What sentence?" Tish finally asked.

"Just something Sheldon wanted taken out."

"Ooooh, what?" begged Nina. "What was it? I bet it was the best part."

Marcy took a deep breath. "I can't tell you."

"Why not? What's the big mystery?" It was Tish again.

"Well, Tish," said Alison, in her quiet way, "if Marcy can't tell us, it must be confidential." But even Alison looked as if she'd like to know. She turned to Marcy. "*Is* it confidential?"

"Yes," Marcy replied. She hated to disappoint Alison, but she wouldn't have liked herself if she had betrayed Sheldon.

"I still don't get all the mystery," Tish complained. "The *Linden Acres Express* prints the truth, the whole truth and nothing but the truth."

Diana said, "Tish is right. Are we going to let Mr. Great-and-Famous tell us how to run our newspaper?"

Even Alison said maybe they shouldn't publish any interviews. Too controversial.

Marcy's heart sank. There went her job on the *Linden Acres Express*, to say nothing of explaining to Sheldon, and Mrs. Weissman's fifty copies.

Mrs. Weissman's fifty copies? Hmmmm! "I just hate to see us lose all that money," she said.

"Money?" echoed Tish. "What money?"

"Sheldon's grandmother ordered fifty copies so

she could send Sheldon's interview to all her friends."

"Fifty copies!" Diana collapsed on the table.

"Fifty *copies*? Or fifty *subscriptions*?" It was Tish again. That girl was really sharp. Copies were fifteen cents, but subscriptions were one dollar. Some difference!

"Copies," Marcy admitted reluctantly.

Alison snatched up a pencil and did some quick figuring. "Well, even so, that's seven dollars and fifty cents, Tish," she said. "We can't very well sneeze at seven dollars and fifty cents, can we?"

"Certainly not," declared Nina, quick as always to agree with Alison. "Why, I think it's wonderful. After all, our biggest issue last year was only twenty-three copies. And here Marcy has sold fifty all by herself. I think we owe her a vote of thanks."

"So do I," agreed Diana. "Even if Tish doesn't."

Tish's mouth dropped open in hurt surprise. "I didn't say I didn't. What did I say? Did I say I didn't?"

"I don't care what you said, Tish Chandlor!" Nina retorted. "I just think we should all thank Marcy for selling fifty copies of the *Linden Acres Express*."

"Let's take a vote," Alison suggested. "All those in favor of printing Marcy's interview raise their hands." Raising her own hand, Alison added softly, "Aye."

Naturally, everyone followed suit. With a girl as popular as Alison Bamforth, who wouldn't?

That afternoon after school Nina asked if she could come over to see Marcy's house, and Marcy said yes.

First Marcy introduced Nina to her mother, then she showed Nina through the downstairs rooms. After that she took her upstairs and showed her the master bedroom and bath, the guest bedroom, the bedroom for the baby, the hall bathroom and, last, her own room.

Nina took in Marcy's bed and her desk and her collection of books. Then her eye fell on a framed photograph hanging on the wall.

"Who's that?" she asked.

"My mom and my dad and me."

Nina studied the photograph more closely. "Was that taken before the divorce?"

"Yes," Marcy replied.

"It looks like you were just a little baby then."

"I was."

"I think your father is handsome. A handsome man."

"Thank you," Marcy said.

"Do you miss him a lot, your dad?"

"Sure."

This Nina was one nosy girl. Marcy watched her look around the room some more. "What's all this about?" she asked, reading a single sheet of notebook paper tacked to Marcy's corkboard. "All those names on this piece of paper."

On one side of the paper Marcy had printed the word "MOM" in capital letters, and on the other side, "DAD." Underneath, she had started two columns of likely names for their babies. She added to the list as she thought of a good one.

When Marcy explained what she was doing, Nina said, "I see you've got Alison down twice. Once on your mom's side, and once on your dad's."

"I like that name a lot."

"But suppose your mom and your dad each have girls and each pick Alison. You'll have two relatives named the same."

Marcy hadn't considered this possibility. Think fast, brains, she told herself. Think fast. "Alison Compton and Alison Benson. That's not the same."

"I still think it's dumb."

"Well, I don't."

She was trying to be friends with Nina, but she had to stand up for herself.

Maybe Nina was trying to be friends, too; because right away she said, "I really like your room."

"Thank you," Marcy replied, and added, "your room is really nice, too, I bet." Then she said, "Come on downstairs and I'll fix us something to eat."

When they were sitting at the table in the breakfast nook, drinking milk and eating chocolate chip cookies, Nina said, "Alison really likes you. She used to like Tish best, but now she likes you best."

Marcy could scarcely believe her ears. "How do you know?"

"She took your side against Tish. About that interview."

"That was just because of all the copies Sheldon's grandmother wants to buy."

"No, it wasn't," Nina insisted. "Maybe it was a little because of that. But mostly it was because she likes you. I like you, too. Everybody does, except Tish. But don't pay any attention to her. She's just mad because Alison doesn't like her best anymore."

"I like everybody," Marcy said.

"Who do you like the best?"

"Well — Alison."

Nina's head bobbed. "Everybody does. I just

love the way her hair goes. And she's not stuck-up, or anything. She's a really popular girl."

After that, they talked about Diana. "A very nice girl," Marcy said. "And a good friend, too," Nina added. Then they talked about the boys in their class. Or mostly Nina talked about them because Marcy said she didn't know the boys well enough.

"How about Rickie Harris?" Nina persisted.

Rickie Harris rode the Blue bus and was in Mr. Willis's homeroom. In Marcy's opinion, he was the nicest boy in the whole school.

"He's fine," she told Nina.

"Fine!" Nina exploded. "Rickie Harris is a lot better than *fine*! Just about every girl in the fifth grade thinks he's perfect!"

"Well, I just got here, don't forget."

Nina looked at her through narrowed eyes. "You know Sheldon the Show-off. What about him?"

Marcy caught her breath. Sheldon the Show-off! Was that what people were calling him? Not that she could altogether blame them, but she said loyally, "He's smart, Nina. Really, really smart."

"*And* he knows it," Nina observed coldly. "Haven't you seen the way he gets this stuck-up smile on his face and looks all around the room

57

when nobody else has the answer? Then he puts his hand up. Yuk! I really feel sorry for you, living on the same street with that creep."

The next day, waiting on the corner with Sheldon, Marcy said, "Sheldon, you shouldn't smile all around the room just because you're the only one that knows an answer. People don't like it."

"How do you know?" Sheldon asked.

"I just know," Marcy replied firmly.

"Well, I've got news for you, Marcy. People around here wouldn't like me no matter what I did."

"Why wouldn't they?"

"Because I've got brains to jingle, that's why."

"What's that got to do with it?"

"People don't like people being smarter than they are. It's prejudice."

"What's 'prejudice'?"

"Look it up. Your word for the day."

Oooh! After this remark Marcy decided she wouldn't say another word. When they reached the school she didn't even remind him, as she sometimes had to do, to get off the bus. But when Mr. Willis asked if anyone could tell the class something about Genghis Khan, she couldn't help noticing that Sheldon didn't smile and look all around. He simply raised his hand.

9

By the end of September, Marcy couldn't believe she had been at the John Wellington Elementary School for only a few weeks.

"I can't believe it!" she told her father over the telephone one night. "It's like I've always been here!"

And somehow it did seem as though she had been living on Dell Lane forever. She really liked her school and her new friends, and when the first issue of the *Linden Acres Express* came out it was a big success. Seventy-five copies were sold, including Mrs. Weissman's fifty, for a grand total of eleven dollars and twenty-five cents.

Marcy was proud of it, especially the page with her interview with Sheldon: "New Neighbor," by Marcia Benson. But she was proud of the other features too: Diana's Sports Page, and the "Dear Alison" column, and Tish Chandlor's cartoon "Linden Loonies," and Nina's TV review. The whole thing looked really great. Tish's father had run it off on the copier in his law office and the girls had stapled the pages together. Everybody liked it a lot, except for — who else? — Sheldon Weissman-hyphenated-Cobb.

"Mistakes, Marcy," he said. "Mistakes in spelling, punctuation. All through it. I'd be ashamed. The Benson byline was the only piece without error. It was a pleasure to read, Marcy. A pleasure."

Marcy didn't know whether to feel good or bad. But clearly Sheldon didn't expect a response. He held out a large manila envelope. "I have a manuscript I'd like to ask you to submit to your editorial board for consideration for publication."

Marcy heaved a sigh. Manuscript. Editorial board. Consideration for publication. Sheldon, pretending to be the great and famous writer again. "A manuscript, Sheldon?"

Sheldon nodded. "I've been thinking the *Linden Acres Express* could use a little fiction to liven things up. I've been thinking your readers might enjoy 'The Invisible Footprint.'"

"Sheldon, in case you haven't noticed, the *Linden Acres Express* is written by girls. By girls *only*."

"Sex discrimination, Marcy. That's against the law. Besides," he added, and there came that smile, "if you print my story, Ellen will want to buy fifty more copies. You might just mention that to your friends."

At the meeting of the *Linden Acres Express* that afternoon in the Bamforths' family room, the first order of business was what to do with eleven dollars and twenty-five cents.

Tish suggested that they should give a bonus to themselves of two dollars and twenty-five cents each. Nina thought they should send the money to the starving people of the world. Alison said, "I think the *Linden Acres Express* should use the money to open its own bank account, with its own deposit slips and everything." Right away everybody agreed to that and they got to work on the next issue.

Diana said for her sports page she wanted to do, "Animals — Give Them A Home/Give Them A Chance."

"Animals!" exclaimed Nina. "Animals aren't a sport!"

"They need a home!" Diana retorted.

"And if it's a dog, you have to exercise it," Marcy pointed out, thinking Diana's suggestion was a good one. "You can jog with it."

"How about jogging?" Tish cried. "A feature on jogging!"

"Jogging isn't a sport, either," declared Nina.

"Well, if it's not a sport, what is it?" Tish shouted hotly.

"It's just jogging," Nina shouted back. Alison picked up her father's hammer and pounded on the block of wood.

After this they all settled down and helped Nina with her entertainment feature: "Treat Your Parents To A Romantic Dinner at Home." (Put candles on the table. Make your mom some kind of corsage. Play romantic music. Serve tuna fish salad, with ginger ale for champagne.)

Tish would do another one of her cartoons, and Marcy was to interview Mr. Willis, "Teacher of John Wellington's Fine Fifth Grade."

They saved the best part for last — dreaming up some really good "Dear Alison" problems.

" 'Dear Alison,' " Tish began. " 'My sister's boyfriend always drives up to the house and honks his horn for her to come out. I think this is rude. What should I do?' Signed, 'Hates Honks.' And the answer is, 'Dear Hates Honks, Buy a goose that will honk back.' "

"Honk!" giggled Alison.

"Honk! Honk!" echoed Nina.

Suddenly everyone was shouting, Honk! Honk! Honk! Honk!

"I wonder where I left my honk?" Diana cried, and everyone screamed, laughing.

Someone said, "I can't understand my honkwork!"

Someone said, "Talk louder, I can't honk you."

Someone said, "Oooo! I have to go to the honk!"

Honk! Honk! Honk! Honk! Everyone kept shouting and giggling until the door at the top of the stairs opened and Mrs. Bamforth called down, "All right, girls. Quiet down."

As soon as the door closed, Marcy said, "Guess what? Sheldon wants us to put one of the stories he wrote in the *Express*."

This quieted everyone down fast.

"He says if we do," she added, "his grandmother will probably buy fifty more copies."

Tish was the first to recover. "That's a bribe!" she exclaimed. "Can the *Linden Acres Express* be bribed?"

Nobody else said anything, so Marcy began to hope that maybe it could. "It's a good story," she continued. "It's called 'The Invisible Footprint.' It's kind of — well, weird."

Everybody burst out laughing, and Nina shouted, "Weird! Look who wrote it!"

"Yes! Look who wrote it!" cried Diana. "And anyway, we don't want boys."

Tish giggled. "Except maybe Rickie Harris."

"Rickie Harris . . . !" caroled Nina, and pretended to swoon.

"But not Sheldon!" Diana insisted. "He's so stuck-up. He acts like he knows everything."

"We could use a paper carrier, though," Alison said, in her calm, practical way. "Marcy, do you think Sheldon would be our paper carrier if we agree to publish his story?"

"Sure!" Marcy exclaimed. "Sure he would!"

"Not just paper carrier for *one* time," Tish put in quickly. "*All* the time. He'll have to promise to carry papers *all* the time."

"Sure," Marcy said.

"And," Diana added, "his grandmother will have to promise to buy at least fifty copies of that issue."

"At least," Nina declared.

Alison looked at Marcy. "Do you think Sheldon and his grandmother would be willing to do all that?"

"Sure!" Marcy replied. "Why not?"

On her way home from Alison's, Marcy stopped by the Weissman residence.

Mrs. Weissman opened the door. In one hand she held a long black cigarette holder, but there was no cigarette in it.

"Mrs. Weissman," Marcy said, "if we agree to put Sheldon's story in the *Linden Acres Express*, will you promise to buy fifty copies?"

"Oh, indeed!" Mrs. Weissman exclaimed. "All my friends will want to read it. That child is a genius." She put the empty cigarette holder between her lips, took a drag on it, removed it, and then blew out a little gust of air. "I've given up smoking, as you see," she said. "It worries Sheldon."

"Is Sheldon home?" Marcy asked.

"Oh, indeed! Just step inside, dear. He's playing with Monty. I'll fetch him."

Marcy had become familiar enough with the Weissman household to understand that Monty was not a person, but a portable computer that Sheldon was challenging to a game of Scrabble.

When he came down the hall, Marcy said, "You can get 'The Invisible Footprint' in the *Linden Acres Express* if you deliver our newspapers for us."

"Whaaat?" Sheldon exclaimed, and glared at her.

Marcy was surprised. "So what's wrong with delivering newspapers?"

"Marcy," Sheldon said, "I am a writer, an author. Do authors deliver newspapers?"

Marcy sighed. With Sheldon, nothing was ever easy. "Sheldon . . ." she began.

"Well, do they?" Sheldon persisted indignantly. "Does my mother have to deliver her books of poems? Does my father have to deliver his books of philosophy? The answer to that is no. No, they do not. Writers think, writers write, writers create. No one asks them to deliver anything. No one would dare."

"Then you can't get your story in the *Linden Acres Express*, Sheldon."

"And do you think I care? Do you think I care about appearing in that sorry excuse for a newspaper?"

"I'll tell them," Marcy said.

"Tell them what?"

"That you don't want to."

Sheldon took a deep breath and blew out a gust of air — rather like his grandmother, only without the empty cigarette holder. "I bet," he said darkly, "your friends would snap it up if that story were by Rickie-Tickie Harris."

"Check," Marcy replied.

"Ole Rickie-Tickie, who couldn't write a story to save his life."

"So what else is new?"

He shook his head in bafflement. "It's such a good story."

"That's not the only thing that counts, Sheldon."

"Why not?" Sheldon demanded.

"People have to like you."

"That should have nothing whatever to do with it."

"Well," Marcy snapped, "it does."

Marcy had scarcely opened her own front door when the telephone rang. It was Sheldon.

"*Bon soir, ma petite,*" he crooned. "You can tell your friends I'll meet their hilarious demands. It will give them a line or two in my biography, years hence."

"You have to promise to carry all the newspapers every issue, Sheldon," Marcy said. "Not just the one issue with your story in it."

There was a pause, then Sheldon said, less jauntily, "Check."

10

One night when her father called on the telephone, he said, "I'd like to come east next week, Marcy. Think you can get permission for me to visit your school?"

"Sure!" Marcy practically shouted. "Sure!"

As the day of his visit drew closer, she began to get so excited that she was making herself sick. She decided to try not to think about it. But this proved difficult because Nina Hernandez kept saying things like, "Where will your father sleep when he gets here? Where will he eat? Will he get to see the inside of your house? Will you get to show him your room?"

Marcy didn't know the answer to some of these questions herself.

"Where will my dad sleep when he gets here?" she asked her mother.

"I imagine," her mother told her, "he will go to a motel."

"Why can't he sleep in the guest room right here?"

"Because he'll feel more comfortable in a motel."

"The guest room is comfortable."

"Not as comfortable as a motel. Under the circumstances."

Marcy knew what "under the circumstances" meant. It meant on account of the divorce, and all. She knew also that her mother wasn't especially enjoying this conversation, but there were some things Marcy just had to find out.

"Where will I sleep when he's here?" she continued. "At the motel, too?"

"I imagine," said her mother, who seemed to have to imagine a lot about this visit, "I imagine you will stay here, and your father will come back and forth."

"And eat? Where will he eat?"

"I've no idea."

"Will he eat here?"

"No, Marcy."

"Well, will he have to eat all by himself?"

"Heavens, Marcy, I've no idea. I imagine he'll take you out to dinner. But it won't be the end of the world if he has to eat a meal by himself."

It might not be the end of the world, but it seemed to Marcy that her mother had a very short memory after all her talk about people feeling left out. It was clear her mother didn't care one bit about how left out Marcy's father might feel.

"Will I at least be able to bring my father into the house and show him my room?" she inquired severely. "I'd at least like to be able to show my father my room."

She thought she saw her mother's lips almost twitch into a smile, but Mrs. Compton merely replied smoothly, "Yes, Marcy, you most certainly may show your father your room."

When the big day finally arrived, and the school bus drew up in front of the John Wellington Elementary School, Marcy forgot all these problems. There was her father, right where he said he would be, standing by the front door.

Her heart started pounding and she started waving even though he didn't see her. He kept looking for her back and forth along the bus windows while she made a beeline for him and flung herself into his arms.

"I can't believe it! I can't believe it!" she cried.

What she couldn't believe was that her father was really there, his blue eyes bright and glittering just as always.

His arms clamped tight and hard around her, and her nose got squashed against the rough tweed of his jacket. His voice was for real and not coming over a telephone. He was for real.

"Well, it looks like somebody's happy," Mr. Willis said, coming up to them.

Marcy introduced the two men, and they smiled and shook hands. Mrs. Finley, the principal, appeared out of nowhere and Marcy introduced her and thanked her for letting her father visit the school. Alison, Diana, Nina, and Tish were all watching and smiling. Marcy was so happy she thought she would pop.

"Marcy," Mr. Willis said, "before the bell rings, maybe you'd like to give your father a little tour of the school. Maybe Alison will take your things to our room."

Alison stepped forward and took Marcy's jacket and her books, and Marcy took her father's hand and they went into the school together.

She showed him the library, decorated for fall with mobiles of colorful leaves; and the gym and the cafeteria. As they walked through the halls, kids said hi, and she said hi right back.

"Well, Marcy," her father said, "it seems like you're a really popular girl."

At lunchtime, Marcy took her father through the cafeteria line where they each ordered a hamburger. Then Marcy led the way to her table and introduced him to her friends. Her father remembered that Nina had two younger sisters; Diana had two older brothers; Alison had a brother on each side of her whom she called "The Bookends"; and that Tish was an only child. Everybody started giggling because Marcy's father pretended he was only guessing about their families, and getting it right every time.

Marcy could scarcely believe he had remembered so much of what she had told him during their conversations over the telephone. He must have paid attention to every word. She could tell her friends liked him a lot, and that made her proud and happy. But after lunch, at recess, when they were all out in the school yard and her father was jingling loose change in his pocket, he said, out of the blue, "Say, where is Sheldon? I haven't met him yet."

"Oooooh!" cried Nina, and threw herself down on the ground.

"Don't mention him!" Tish exclaimed.

"You mean," asked Diana, "the great Sheldon Weissman-hyphenated-Cobb?"

"Mr. Benson," Alison said quietly, "nobody likes him."

Marcy felt her father's blue eyes fixed on her. "Except me," she made herself say. "I like him."

When she introduced Sheldon, who was by himself as usual on the playground, Sheldon stuck out his hand to her father. "This is a pleasure, Mr. Benson," he said. "A pleasure and a privilege to meet Marcy's father."

Marcy was glad there was nobody else around to hear Sheldon trying to act like he was Mr. Willis, or somebody.

"I'm glad to meet you, too, Sheldon," Mr. Benson said. "Marcia has talked about you a great deal."

Sheldon nodded. "Your daughter is my only friend."

And no wonder! thought Marcy. It interested her that her father really seemed to like Sheldon.

"He's a bright kid," Mr. Benson said as he and Marcy drove off after school that afternoon in the car he had rented at the airport.

Marcy was going to show him Linden Acres Mall and where she went to Sunday school and the Barn Cinema where everybody went to the movies, and places like that.

"The trouble with Sheldon," she said, "is that he's such a show-off. He thinks he knows everything. He doesn't act like other kids."

Marcy would never have said this to Alison, or even to Nina. But somehow she didn't feel guilty complaining about Sheldon to her father.

Mr. Benson chuckled. "I can see where he might get a little obnoxious."

"What's 'obnoxious'?"

"Oh, it means unpleasant, offensive."

"Obnoxious," Marcy repeated. She was really getting into words these days. "That just fits Sheldon Weissman-hyphenated-Cobb."

"But remember," her father cautioned, "that the reason Sheldon doesn't *act* like other kids is because he *isn't* like other kids. He sees things differently."

Marcy didn't understand how her father could know this, but she had another question on her mind. "Do you think I'm like other kids?"

"Not quite," he replied.

"How come?"

"Lots of kids wouldn't have stood up for Sheldon the way you did in the school yard today." He grinned at her across the front seat. "I'm proud of you."

After their tour of all the outdoor places, it was time for Marcy to show her father her room. But a funny thing began to happen. The closer they got to Dell Lane, the quieter it got in the car. By the time they were going up the front walk and into the house, they were hardly speaking at all.

"This is the living room," Marcy said. "This is the dining room. This is the kitchen."

She felt like some kind of nut, announcing what the rooms were when her father could see for himself. But she didn't know what else to say.

It was a big relief to Marcy that her mother wasn't at home so nobody had to make up any pretend conversation. But this felt strange, too, because her mother was usually always around.

Another thing — and this was really creepy — it was almost as though she and her father were trespassing — as though they shouldn't really be in the house at all.

It got a little better when Marcy showed her father her own room. She pointed out the picture of him and her mom and herself that was taken when she was little, and the list of names she was keeping for his new baby.

"I like the name Alison," he said.

Marcy nodded. "That's my favorite."

"I'll mention it to Ginny."

"Sure. See how she likes it. And even if Mom and Step pick that name, too, it's still all right. On account of Alison *Benson* and Alison *Compton*."

Her father nodded. "Different last names."

"Check," Marcy said.

She was glad when she finished showing the house, and they could go off for dinner at the motel where he was staying.

Marcy had pork chops and apple sauce, and her father had steak and a salad.

While they were eating, he told her about Ginny's little boy, Joey, now three years old.

"Does Joey still say 'Who you?' " Marcy asked.

"He does. To everyone he sees. And another thing he says all the time is, 'Where's Marcy?' "

"He does?"

"Yes, indeed. He missed you after you left this summer. He cried and wanted us to make you come back."

"Tell him I'll be back! You tell him I'll be back to play with him all summer!"

"I'll tell him," her father said. His smile deepened. "You'll have to help us take care of little what's-its-name, too."

By next summer, the Benson-Comptons would have a new little kid on each coast. Marcy could see she was going to be busy. "Sure I will!" she promised.

And then her father said something that really surprised her. He said he would be going home the very next day.

"You're going home tomorrow!" Marcy cried.

"I can't stay any longer, Marcy. I wish I could."

"But I thought . . . I mean, what about your business? I thought you came to do some business."

He shook his head. "No business. This trip was just to see you."

"Just to see me?"

"To see you, and to see your new school, and what your new friends look like, and your new room."

She could scarcely believe her ears. "You came all the way from San Francisco just for that?"

"Sure. Now, when we talk on the telephone, I'll have a mental image in my mind's eye."

Marcy was blinking so fast she could hardly see. "Dad," she said, "I keep a mental image in my mind's eye of you, too."

11

The day after Mr. Benson's visit was a Thursday, and it rained.

The rain put Marcy in a bad humor. So did wishing it was still yesterday when her father was with her, and worrying about him maybe getting killed in an airplane crash flying back to San Francisco.

But Marcy's mother put Marcy in the worst humor of all. When Marcy got down to breakfast, Mrs. Compton didn't say one word about how nice it was that Marcy's father had come all the way from California, just to see his daughter. Her mother didn't say, How was your father? or Did you have a nice time? She didn't seem to be thinking about anything except fixing Mr. Compton's scrambled eggs.

"I don't want anything to eat this morning," Marcy said coldly. She knew she was being ob-

78

noxious, but she didn't care. "You don't have to fix me anything to eat at all."

Instead of her mother refusing to permit this; instead of her mother refusing to let her daughter spend an entire morning without a thing in her stomach, Mrs. Compton merely said, "All right, dear."

"I don't want to be called dear," Marcy said.

She was really surprised when she said this and she waited to be punished for talking fresh. But her mother pretended not to hear. Marcy knew she was pretending. Probably her mother didn't care whether Marcy talked fresh or not, now that she was pregnant and would soon have a new kid to care for.

But one thing was sure, Marcy decided: If the baby was a girl, she wasn't going to suggest it be called Alison.

Marching up the stairs to her room, she took a black crayon from her box of art supplies and drew a heavy line over the name *Alison* on her mother's side of the list. Only her father and Ginny's baby would get the chance to be called that, if Marcy had any say in the matter.

Just thinking about her father being right in this room only yesterday, and now being in an airplane traveling away from her faster than the speed of sound, brought tears she could no longer hold back. Marcy sat down on the edge of her bed, dropped her face in her hands, and cried.

When she got back downstairs, she knew her mother and Mr. Compton could tell she had been crying. But they went right on eating and Marcy was glad they didn't ask her what was the matter, or say a word.

"Could I have some breakfast, please?" she asked politely.

"Certainly, dear." Her mother got up from the table right away.

As soon as Marcy finished a plate of delicious scrambled eggs, she hurried upstairs, took a fresh sheet of paper, and wrote up a new list of names. She put Alison back on her mother's side, just where it had always been. Marcy was feeling much better, and she was really glad that when she had been obnoxious her mother had pretended not to hear.

The October issue of the *Linden Acres Express* came out at the end of the month. It was a financial success. Ninety-two copies were sold for a grand total of thirteen dollars and eighty cents.

The increase in circulation was due not only to the sale of fifty copies to Ellen Weissman, but to the fact that Sheldon himself had sold an additional seventeen.

"How did you do it?" Marcy exclaimed.

"I simply went around the neighborhood and knocked on people's doors," Sheldon replied. "I pointed out that this was a local newspaper, written by local residents, and asked homeowners if they felt they could afford to be without it."

Marcy had sold the *Express* to her father and to her step, just as the other girls had sold subscriptions to their families and friends. She knew, however, that none of them would have gone around knocking on strangers' doors the way Sheldon did. The staff of the *Express*, even Tish, was now more than happy to have him "on the team," as Alison said.

In fact, after the October issue, Marcy could see things loosening up for Sheldon. Rickie Harris read "The Invisible Footprint" and told everybody it was good. And Alison took to calling Sheldon "Shel," and being more friendly, so naturally a certain number of people picked up on that. But Sheldon still stayed by himself on the school playground and lots of times kids would call out, "Shelly-belly! Yoo-hoo, Shelly-belly!"

"Pay no attention, Marcy," Sheldon advised her when it happened as they were walking out of the Barn Cinema one Saturday afternoon. "Someday I shall be a great and famous writer."

Marcy figured that since Sheldon intended to

be great and famous someday, he probably didn't care whether people liked him right now. It certainly seemed that way when, one day in early November, he invited Marcy to go along with Ellen Weissman and him to the Museum of Natural History on the coming Sunday afternoon.

"I can't," Marcy regretfully told him, as they stood waiting for the school bus. "My relatives are coming to visit."

"What relatives?" Sheldon inquired.

"Mr. Compton's mother and father."

Sheldon frowned. "They aren't your relatives, Marcy. They are no relation to you at all. They are your mother's in-laws. Period. When old Reddi-Whip's people used to come to visit, I would go into my room, lock the door, and not come out all day."

"Why would you do that?"

"Because as far as they were concerned, I didn't exist. I might as well have been painted on the wall. They scarcely even looked at me."

"Maybe if you were nice to them, they would have."

"Why should I be nice to them? Why should I want to hang around and listen to all their boring talk about their wonderful son?"

Marcy couldn't imagine going to her room and

locking the door when the senior Comptons came to call. "What did your mom do?" she asked. "When you wouldn't come out of your room, I mean."

"What could she do?" demanded Sheldon.

"Well, what did your step do?"

"What could he do? Break down the door?"

"Maybe," Marcy said, "that's why he doesn't want you to live in his place. One of the reasons, I mean."

"So, who cares about living in his place? It's a dumb place. Marcy, when my mother and I moved in with him, there wasn't one book in his whole apartment — not one. Only sports magazines and TV sets. Great big TV sets in every room. And telephones. Even in the bathrooms."

"He must be rich, I bet."

"Rich and stupid. For the life of me, I'll never know what my mother sees in him. After being married to a genius like my father, too! You talk about books. You should see my father's place. Books everywhere." Sheldon's eyes got this far-away look. "That's the one thing I can remember about my father's place. All the books."

"Well, anyway, Sheldon, I still can't go on Sunday," Marcy said.

"Maybe you could, Marcy. You might be able to. Ask your mom."

Marcy shook her head. "I'd hurt Step's feelings. If I didn't stay and help out, I mean."

"But he's not your real father. He's only your stepfather. Stepfather."

Marcy thought of Mr. Compton helping her with her arithmetic. She thought of him driving her to Sunday school. She thought of him rapping on her door each morning and singing out, "Rise and shine."

"I like him," she said.

"You do?" Sheldon exclaimed, like he couldn't believe his ears.

"Sure. I think he's nice."

"Hmmmm," he mumbled thoughtfully. "Hmmmm."

More and more these days, Sheldon seemed to be at a loss for words.

12

It was decided that the baby's room would be painted yellow. Marcy helped paint it, being especially careful with the brush going around the white trim. It really looked cheerful when they got finished and put up the decals of kittens and butterflies. Marcy's mother made yellow curtains with a pattern of little orange flowers, and one night Mr. Compton came home carrying a huge rocking chair.

"Bill!" Marcy's mother cried, laughing. "That's too big for the baby's room!"

"You can put it in my room!" Marcy offered quickly.

"Marcy," her mother said, "you won't want a big rocking chair in your pretty room."

"Sure I will," Marcy insisted. "Alie will like getting rocked in it."

It had been decided that, if a girl, the baby

would be called Alison, and if a boy, Alan. This way, Marcy had pointed out, they could talk about Alie, and play it safe either way.

The rocking chair ended up in the baby's room after all. When the decision came down to a family vote, Marcy sided with her step and that made two against one.

Sometimes she would go in and rock in it, getting in practice even though Alie wouldn't be born until March. She could hardly wait.

With her new school, her new friends, and two new babies on the way, Marcy figured, she should have known things were too good to last.

"That's life," Mr. Compton sometimes said. "A little bit of sun, a little bit of rain. . . ."

And if there was anyone who could be counted upon to bring a little bit of rain, it was Sheldon Weissman-hyphenated-Cobb.

It all started out nicely enough.

Sheldon had sent a copy of the October issue of the *Linden Acres Express* to his father. His father had read "The Invisible Footprint" and then called his son, saying he would like to visit him. Sheldon had responded by inviting his father to come to Parents' Night at the John Wellington Elementary School, in two weeks.

"Oooooh!" caroled Nina, when Marcy reported this news. "Is his mom coming to Parents' Night, too? I mean, is it going to be his dad and his mom and his step, all here at the same time?"

The staff of the *Linden Acres Express* was gathered in the Bamforths' family room to plan the November issue.

"Well, Nina," Alison said, "why shouldn't they all be here? I don't see any reason why they shouldn't all be here, if they want to be."

"Maybe," Diana offered, "Sheldon's step will be busy and have to stay in New York City, and just his mom will come. They'll sit together — Sheldon's mom and his dad, I mean — and talk over old times, and they'll decide to get back together again."

Marcy shook her head. "I don't think they'll ever get back together again."

"Why not?" Tish demanded.

Marcy thought of how she used to wish her mom and dad would get back together. "It just doesn't happen that way," she said.

As it turned out, she was right.

"My mom isn't coming to Parents' Night," Sheldon confided a few days later. "On account of my dad being here."

Marcy nodded. "One at a time."

"Sure," Sheldon agreed. And then his voice went kind of funny. "The only thing is, I miss her. I haven't seen her in a long time."

Marcy knew what he meant. When she had been out in San Francisco visiting her dad, she would sometimes get to missing her mom something awful. And here in Linden Acres, it was the same way about missing her dad. The best thing to do when this happened was to turn your mind onto something else.

Think fast, brains, she told herself. Think fast. "Maybe the *Linden Acres Express* could do a story about your dad's visit," she suggested.

Bull's-eye! She could see Sheldon brighten up right away.

"An editorial," he exclaimed. "An editorial welcoming this genius! This great philosopher! Why didn't I think of it myself?"

"I guess you're just not as smart as I am," Marcy said, and smiled a small Sheldon-type smile.

Since Tish had only her "Linden Loonies" cartoon to do, it was decided that she would write the editorial on Sheldon's father. To this end, Sheldon arrived at the school bus stop one morning with a neatly typewritten sheet of paper that contained what he called his father's *curriculum vitae.*

"Curriculum *what?*" Marcy asked.

"It's Latin, Marcia," Sheldon explained. *"Curriculum vitae* — a list of where my father went to school, the degrees he holds, books written, stuff like that."

"Ummm," Marcy murmured. She still didn't always understand what Sheldon was saying, but she knew him better now, and no longer believed he was showing off.

For her part of the November *Express,* it had been decided that she would interview Mrs. Finley, the principal of the John Wellington School. Diana's sports page would feature the local Thanksgiving Day football game, Nina would write a poem about the Puritans and Thanksgiving or about the Puritans and the Indians or both.

At the lunch table in the cafeteria on Friday, Alison said that instead of her "Dear Alison" column, each of the editors should tell the thing they were most thankful for and she would write it up. She turned to Marcy with her nice smile. "Marcia, you start."

Marcy looked around at Nina and Diana and

Tish and Alison. She had wanted to make friends so badly when she came to Linden Acres, and now she was friends with all these girls. "The thing I'm most thankful for," she said, "is having friends."

13

Marcy had almost forgotten about Mr. Compton's "little bit of sun, a little bit of rain" until Saturday morning when Sheldon stood in the kitchen of the Compton residence. He held up for her inspection the editorial Tish had written welcoming his father to Linden Acres.

"Look at it, Marcy!" he commanded. "Just look at it! When I told Tish I would like to see it before publication, I merely wanted to check the facts. But this . . . ! This . . . !"

He shook the paper in fury as Marcy stared at the jumble of words written with felt-tip pen in Tish's slapdash hand. Great circles and slashes made with a blue pencil ran all over the page. She blanched. "Those blue marks. . . . Who made them?"

"Who made them?" Sheldon repeated. "I made them!"

Marcy gulped. "You took Tish's editorial and put those blue marks all over it?"

"Of course I did! I corrected her mistakes, Marcy. Mistakes in grammar, punctuation, spelling. Look, Marcy, look!"

Sheldon slapped Tish's paper down on the kitchen counter and jabbed at a word with his finger. "How do you spell believe? B-e-l-e-i-v-e? or b-e-l-i-e-v-e? There's a very simple rule, known to every birdbrain: i before e, except after c. Obviously, Miss Tish Chandlor has not troubled to learn this rule.

"And here," he continued, jabbing at the page again. "Where she says, 'Dr. Cobb will be staying at the Weissman hoose.' Hoose! What is a hoose, may I ask? Has anyone ever heard of a hoose? Seen a hoose? Lived in a hoose? Sheer carelessness! Any self-respecting first-grader would do better.

"And, Marcy, just look at this," he went on wrathfully. " 'Dr. Cobb has taught english.' " Sheldon shook the paper again. "Small e! Can you believe it? The word English, spelled with a small e? And commas, commas, everywhere! Well, I took them out. I took almost every one of those commas out."

Marcy had been staring in horror at the bright blue slashes that cut across the page. Now she looked up at him. "You've ruined it!" she whispered. "After all Tish's work! You've ruined it!"

Sheldon's mouth dropped open in surprise. "Ruined it? I corrected it. I made it better."

"It wasn't any of your business to make it better, Sheldon!" Marcy countered hotly. "You're not Mr. Willis. This wasn't done for school. Nobody would have minded all those commas or that words were spelled wrong. Everybody likes Tish. She's a really popular girl."

"Who can't spell or punctuate!"

"Who cares?" Marcy demanded.

"I care!" cried Sheldon. "There were errors. You've got to correct errors."

"*You* don't, Sheldon. *You* don't. Because you're not a teacher, Sheldon."

"Who cares?" Sheldon shouted.

"Everybody cares," Marcy yelled back at him. She had never been so mad in her life. "Except you, Sheldon. You don't care whose feelings you hurt because you're obnoxious, Sheldon. Obnoxious. Look it up! Your word for the day."

Mrs. Compton came into the kitchen. "Good heavens!" she said. "What's happening?"

Marcy and Sheldon looked at her as though she had dropped from the sky. Sheldon recovered himself first. "Mrs. Compton," he said, "I apologize for causing a disturbance in your house."

Then he picked up Tish's paper from the kitchen counter and marched out the back door.

"Marcy, what in the world has happened?" her mother asked.

"The editorial Tish wrote to welcome Sheldon's father . . . ," Marcy spluttered. "Sheldon put blue pencil marks all over it!"

"But why?"

"Because of mistakes, that's why! Too many commas, he says, and wrong spellings, and . . . and. . . ." She was so mad she could hardly speak. "Sheldon Weissman-hyphenated-Cobb is a know-it-all and a show-off!"

"But was he right?" her mother asked.

"It doesn't matter whether he was right or not!" Marcy replied.

But she could tell that her mother thought it did.

That night the telephone at the Comptons' house kept ringing and ringing. First Nina called to say that Sheldon had given Tish back her editorial with blue markings all over it, that it was ruined, and it was just a shame. Then Diana called to say the same thing. Alison called and said that Tish was very upset and that she, Alison, felt very sorry for her. She said that Tish had promised to bring the editorial to school tomorrow and show it to them at lunchtime. Finally, Tish herself called to say she was sure Marcy could never understand how she, Tish, felt about what had happened because Marcy and Sheldon Weissman-Cobb were such good friends.

"I'm not his friend," Marcy told her.

"I thought you were," Tish responded.

"No," Marcy said firmly. "Not anymore."

14

When Marcy got to the bus stop the next morning she found Sheldon already there.

"Hi," he said.

"I'm not talking to you, Sheldon," she told him. "I'm mad at you for what you did to Tish. And I'm not sitting with you on the bus."

"So who cares?" Sheldon said. "Who cares?"

When the school bus came, Marcy hopped on and scanned the seats real fast. Make someone be absent, make someone be absent, she prayed.

Someone was. Toward the back she saw an empty place next to a girl named Danielle Walters. The seat was usually taken by a girl named Beth Aronson, who got on at an earlier stop.

"May I sit here today?" Marcy asked.

Danielle looked surprised. "Be my guest."

Marcy felt she owed an explanation. "I don't want to sit with Sheldon Weissman-Cobb."

Danielle gave a loud snicker. "Who would?"

When Alison got on at Myrtle Way and spied Marcy sitting beside Danielle instead of beside Sheldon, she smiled approvingly and waved her hand. When Nina and Diana and Tish got on, they smiled and waved, too. When the bus reached the John Wellington Elementary School, Marcy's friends got out and stood on the pavement waiting for her.

It may have been because Marcy had her eyes on her friends that she didn't notice Sheldon wasn't getting off the bus. But by lunchtime everybody, even the teachers, were laughing. Word had gotten around that Sheldon had ridden all the way over to the depot by the shopping center before the bus driver discovered him and brought him back.

"What a nut!" kids were saying. "What a dumb-dumb!" And in the halls they were strumming their lips at him and going *"dah, dah, dah"*; and they were going, "Shelly-belly! Yoo hoo, Shelly-belly!"

They were making Marcy good and mad. Then at the lunch table in the cafeteria Tish passed her marked-up editorial around.

"Oooooh!" Nina cried. "Look what he did to it!"

"Yipes!" Diana exclaimed.

"Who does he think he is?" It was Nina again.

"Poor Tish," Alison said. "Poor Tish."

"I'll have to write the whole thing all over again," Tish wailed.

"I don't think Tish should have to do it all over," Nina declared. "Who cares about Sheldon Weissman-Cobb's genius father? I don't think the *Linden Acres Express* should publish it at all."

"But wasn't he right?" Marcy asked. She was angry at the way everybody was ganging up on Sheldon and she realized her mother had asked her the same question yesterday.

"It doesn't matter whether he's right or not," Diana snapped.

"I think it does," Marcy said.

After lunch Marcy saw Sheldon standing off by himself in the playground. Every now and then some kid would dance by him, strumming his lips and going "*dah, dah, dah.*"

"I'm going to talk to Sheldon for a while," she said.

Nobody tried to stop her. She had a feeling the girls didn't want her around.

"I think we should make up," she told Sheldon.

Sheldon gave a nod. "Okay," he said.

Danielle Walters came up to them, together with a girl named Nan Hefner. "Nan wants you to sit with her on the bus," Danielle told Marcy. "There's an empty seat beside her. I mean," Danielle continued, "unless I can get Beth Aronson to sit with Nan. Because I'd like you to sit with me." She jerked a thumb at Sheldon. "Unless you're going back to sitting with him."

"I'm going back to sitting with him," Marcy said.

"Well, just remember, you're always welcome." Danielle leaned toward Marcy. "Rickie Harris wants you to sit with him, too," she whispered. Turning, she yelled across the playground, "Rickie! Rickie Harris! Here she is. She's right here."

Marcy saw Rickie look over at her and kind of wave his hand. She kind of waved back.

She saw Nina and Diana and Tish and Alison look over at her, too.

That night the Compton's telephone started ringing again. Alison called to say that since Sheldon was selling so many newspapers they were going to publish the editorial with his corrections. She had offered to copy it over because it wouldn't be fair for Tish to have to do the whole thing twice. What did Marcy think of that?

Marcy said she thought that would be great, and that it was really nice of Alison to do a thing like that.

Then Alison asked if Marcy liked Danielle Walters better than she liked Nina and Diana and Tish and herself. Marcy said she liked Danielle, but she still liked her old friends best; especially Alison, because Alison always tried to be nice to everyone.

Nina called and said pretty much the same thing, then she asked if Marcy knew that Rickie Harris liked her. Marcy said that she did. Nina said Marcy was a lucky girl.

Marcy called Tish to tell her that she was really glad her editorial was going to be in the *Linden Acres Express*. She said it was good Alison was going to copy it over because it wouldn't be fair for Tish to have to do the whole thing twice.

A few minutes later Diana called to say that it had been really nice of Marcy to call Tish because that made Tish feel better about the whole thing.

When Marcy hung up after talking to Diana she started to dial Sheldon's number, but her mother called from the living room. "That's enough for tonight, Marcy. Not another phone call."

Marcy went over and stood in the doorway. "But I've got something I need to tell Sheldon."

"Tell him tomorrow," her mother said. "And after this, you are permitted only two telephone calls a night, going out or coming in."

"Except for my father," Marcy said quickly. "It doesn't count when I talk to my father."

"No, Marcy, it won't count when you talk to your father. But pass the word to everyone else."

Mr. Compton was tuning the TV. He looked across the room at his wife and grinned. "Sweetheart," he said, "it sounds to me like we've got ourselves a really popular girl."

15

The first thing Marcy said when she joined Sheldon at the bus stop the next morning was, "Tish's editorial is going to be in the *Linden Acres Express* the way you fixed it."

"No, Marcy, it's not," Sheldon responded. He handed her a long white envelope. "I would like you to present this letter to your editorial board. It's a request that the editorial be withdrawn from publication because my father isn't coming."

"Not coming!"

"He called last night. He has to go to Australia."

"Australia!"

"He's been invited to lecture at a university there. It's a very important invitation, a great honor."

After a moment, Marcy said, "I'm sorry he's not coming to Parents' Night, Sheldon. I really am."

Sheldon gave a shrug. "So who cares?" he said, but Marcy could tell from his voice that he did care. "I didn't really want him to come anyway," Sheldon insisted.

Marcy nodded. "Sure," she said.

"Just a lot of fuss and bother."

"Sure."

"So who needs it?"

"Check."

"Who cares?"

"Right."

"Anyway. . . ." He shrugged his shoulders again. "Well, anyway, my mom's going to come, instead."

"To Parents' Night?"

Sheldon nodded. "Step is coming, too."

Marcy had never heard Sheldon call his stepfather anything but "old Reddi-Whip." Things were getting more interesting all the time.

"I might even go back with them," Sheldon added.

"To New York City?"

"Yep."

"To visit?"

Sheldon was smiling. "Nope. To stay."

Marcy was really surprised. "Will your step let you?"

"He wants me to."

"Maybe he likes you. Deep down, I mean."

"It's hard to see why."

"People around here were getting to like you. Until you went and hurt Tish's feelings, that is."

Sheldon nodded. "I was wrong about that. Not about the corrections. But I went about things the wrong way."

Marcy could scarcely believe her ears. "You admit it!"

"Marcy," Sheldon said, "no one has ever accused me of failing to admit a mistake."

Standing on the corner beside him, Marcy tried to get used to the idea that Sheldon might not be around Linden Acres much longer. Whom would she talk to in the mornings as she waited for the school bus? Who would sell extra copies of the *Linden Acres Express*? Who would write stories like "The Invisible Footprint"? Who would care how words got spelled?

And, now she thought of it, who would care about Sheldon Weissman-hyphenated-Cobb in his new school in New York City? Who would make sure he got off the school bus? Be his friend?

"I'll write to you, Sheldon," she said. "And you can call me on the telephone any time you want."

Marcy was glad she had thought to say this. A telephone call from Sheldon was sure to count in her mother's new rule about incoming/outgoing calls. But she figured Sheldon might need somebody like her.

The school bus rounded the corner, its blinking yellow lights changing to blinking red. Marcy hopped on, followed by Sheldon.

"Let's sit here," she said. Sheldon sat down beside her and the bus moved off.

Gazing out the window at streets and houses now grown familiar, Marcy wondered where she would sit after Sheldon left for New York City. Maybe with Danielle Walters or Nan Hefner. Maybe with Nina or Alison. Or even Rickie Harris. One thing for sure, she wasn't going to worry about it. It wouldn't be like her first day at John Wellington two months ago. Back then, she had been so scared and nervous. But now . . . well, as her step said last night, it looked like she had become a really popular girl.

APPLE®PAPERBACKS

More books you'll love, filled with mystery, adventure, friendship, and fun!

NEW APPLE TITLES

- ☐ 40284-6 **Christina's Ghost** Betty Ren Wright **$2.50**
- ☐ 41839-4 **A Ghost in the Window** Betty Ren Wright **$2.50**
- ☐ 41794-0 **Katie and Those Boys** Martha Tolles **$2.50**
- ☐ 40565-9 **Secret Agents Four** Donald J. Sobol **$2.50**
- ☐ 40554-3 **Sixth Grade Sleepover** Eve Bunting **$2.50**
- ☐ 40419-9 **When the Dolls Woke** Marjorie Filley Stover **$2.50**

BEST SELLING APPLE TITLES

- ☐ 41042-3 **The Dollhouse Murders** Betty Ren Wright **$2.50**
- ☐ 42319-3 **The Friendship Pact** Susan Beth Pfeffer **$2.75**
- ☐ 40755-4 **Ghosts Beneath Our Feet** Betty Ren Wright **$2.50**
- ☐ 40605-1 **Help! I'm a Prisoner in the Library** Eth Clifford **$2.50**
- ☐ 40724-4 **Katie's Baby-sitting Job** Martha Tolles **$2.50**
- ☐ 40494-6 **The Little Gymnast** Sheila Haigh **$2.50**
- ☐ 40283-8 **Me and Katie (the Pest)** Ann M. Martin **$2.50**
- ☐ 42316-9 **Nothing's Fair in Fifth Grade** Barthe DeClements **$2.75**
- ☐ 40607-8 **Secrets in the Attic** Carol Beach York **$2.50**
- ☐ 40180-7 **Sixth Grade Can Really Kill You** Barthe DeClements **$2.50**
- ☐ 41118-7 **Tough-Luck Karen** Johanna Hurwitz **$2.50**
- ☐ 42326-6 **Veronica the Show-off** Nancy K. Robinson **$2.75**
- ☐ 42374-6 **Who's Reading Darci's Diary?** Martha Tolles **$2.75**

Available wherever you buy books...or use the coupon below.

Scholastic Inc. P.O. Box 7502, 2932 E. McCarty Street, Jefferson City, MO 65102

Please send me the books I have checked above. I am enclosing $_____

(please add $1.00 to cover shipping and handling). Send check or money order—no cash or C.O.D.'s please.

Name _____

Address _____

City _____ State/Zip _____

Please allow four to six weeks for delivery. Offer good in U.S.A. only. Sorry, mail order not available to residents of Canada. Prices subject to change. **APP 888**